Come On

Written by

Illustrated by Audrey Heffner

Copyright © Mary Kristina Paradis
ISBN: 978-0-9971195-1-0

Boom!

Bang!

Come on!

Let's go!

Come on. Let's go.
Let's watch the show.
The heavens are performing.
There's color and light.
This could go on all night.
Who knows when the heavens are storming?

Are you cozy and warm?
We will come to no harm.
God is watering his grass and his flowers.

They've had enough sun.
Now there's work to be done.
This part could go on for just hours.

Aren't the flowers afraid, Mom?
It's so loud and so bright.
Won't this all get too wet, Mom,
If it goes on all night?
It's so messy and blowy,
Just a terrible sight.

Does this mean God is mad, Mom?
I don't think I've been bad, Mom.
Doesn't God love his flowers and trees?
But, the thunder's too loud, Mom.
Too much rain in those clouds, Mom.
Should we ask God to make it stop please?

Now our garden can grow, Dear.
And, the streams can now flow, Dear.
Oh, the rain is a friend, just believe.
Could our gardens now bloom
If there wasn't some boom?
Without rain to refresh and relieve?

Get your slicker and boots.
Just be smart. You'll look cute!
We'll go splashing from puddle to puddle.

The rain is just water
From God's home to ours.
There's really none better
For puddles or flowers!

And just look. Here's the best.
See the sun in the West?
The sun and the rain are like brothers.
When they meet up at last,
And the storm has just passed,...

God mixes them up to make colors!

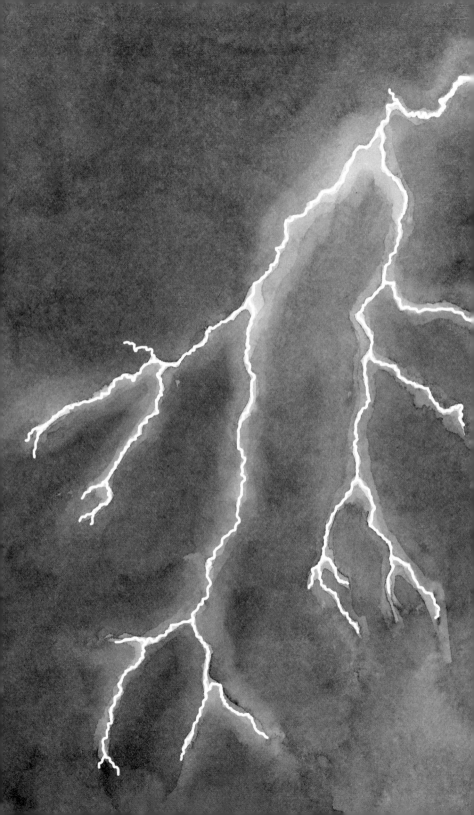

Boom!

Bang!

Come on! Let's go!

CPSIA information can be obtained at www.ICGtesting.com
Printed in the USA
LVIW01n1454270516
490218LV00003B/3